Bunda's Dreaming

AN ORIGINAL STORY BASED ON THE ABORIGINAL DREAMTIME

WRITTEN BY JAY MATHEWS

Rising Stars UK Ltd, 22 Grafton Street, London W1S 4EX

www.risingstars-uk.com

Published 2007
Text, design and layout © Rising Stars UK Ltd.

Series Consultant: Jay Mathews
Cover design: Marmalade Book Design (www.marmaladebookdesign.com)
Design: Marmalade Book Design
Illustrations: David Woodroffe (Chapter One)
Publisher: Gill Budgell

British Library Cataloguing in Publication Data.
A CIP record for this book is available from the British Library.

ISBN: 978-1-84680-368-0

Printed by: Gutenberg Press, Malta

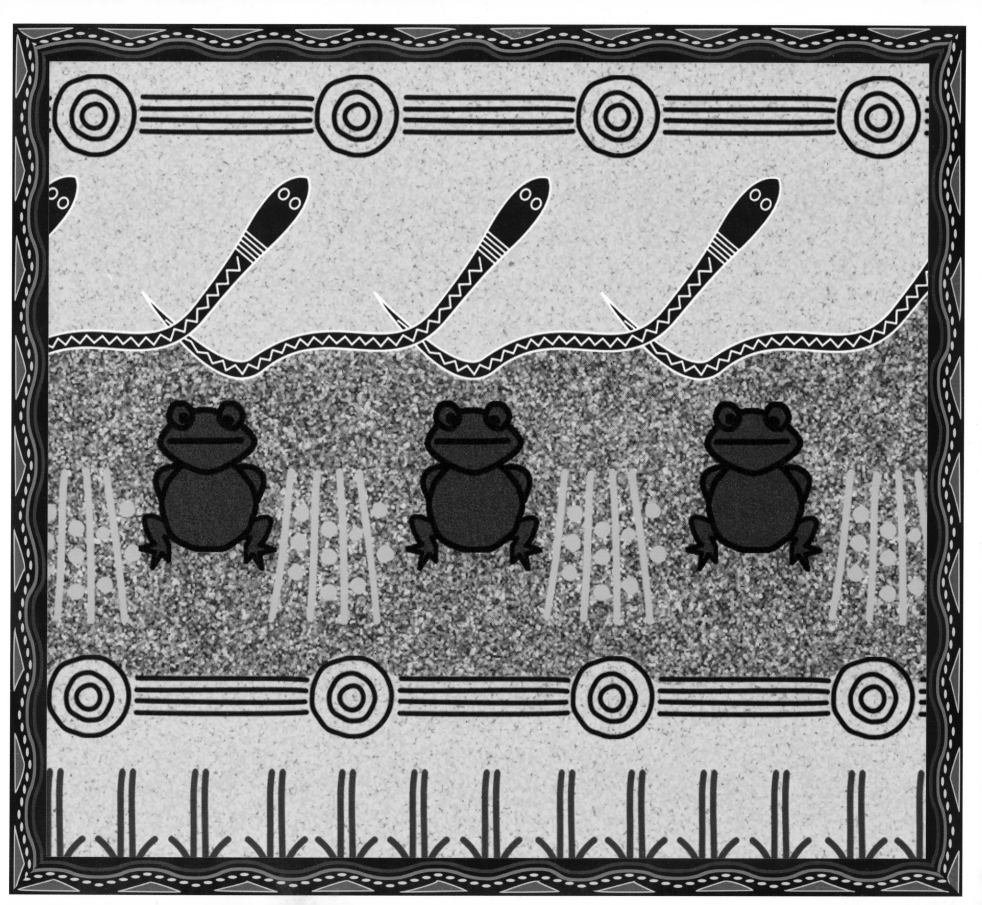

◈ Chapter 1 ◈

Gran Comes to Visit

Streetlights were flickering as they turned on, cutting a misty yellow path through the cold gathering dusk. Alice Nanjmira sat by the window waiting for her grandson to come home from school.

Parents hurried past the house. They were pushing buggies and pulling warmly coated toddlers by the hand as they rushed to get to the school gates to meet their older children from school. It was late January and it was still bitterly cold.

Alice had recently arrived from Australia to visit her family. She was eighty years old and this was her first trip to England.

"It's summer time in Perth," she thought to herself, "I'd be sitting on my porch feeling too hot to even move!"

Alice sighed as she thought about her own home half way round the world. She was enjoying her holiday in England, and it was lovely to be with her family, but she was beginning to miss her friends and the company of her little dog Tizer. A voice, calling out, broke into her dreamings.

"Gran, I'm home!" Bunda, aged eight, catapulted into the room discarding his book bag, coat, shoes and lunch box in a colourful confusion behind him. Flinging himself onto his Gran he gave her a clumsy hug.

"Did you have a good day at school?" asked Gran.

"Yeah great! I told Miss Carter that you'd come all the way from Australia to visit us and she thought it was really cool. We spent ages in 'show and tell' time looking at Australia on the

map and talking about stuff... I'm starving!"

With that, he shot off to the kitchen. Loud banging and clatterings indicated that he was making himself his usual 'coming home from school' snack and probably creating a big mess.

Alice smiled. Bunda was so like her daughter had been at the same age, full of life and energy, with an enormous appetite! She had missed Bunda's mother, Samantha, very badly when she'd come to England to work ten years ago. Now she was a married woman with a husband and a lovely son of her own. Time went so quickly. Sighing softly, Alice returned to her own dreaming.

"Hey Gran!" Bunda had returned, his mouth full of tuna sandwich. He flopped down onto the sofa and eyed her seriously.

"Will you be coming up to tell me another story at bedtime tonight?"

"If you'd like me to," smiled Alice.

"Yesssss!" shouted Bunda, punching the air in excitement.

"Er… Gran?"

Alice knew what was coming. "Yes, Bunda?"

"Will I be getting another one of your presents?"

"Wait and see," said Gran mysteriously!

◈ Chapter 2 ◈

The Rainbow Serpent

Later that same evening Bunda was tucked up in bed. Snuggling luxuriously beneath his duvet, Bunda looked up hopefully at his Gran. Gran laughed at his earnest pleading face.

"Close your eyes and hold out your hands, Bunda," she said.

Screwing his eyes up tight, and holding his breath in anticipation, Bunda held out his hands. A soft piece of material, the size of a tea towel, was placed in them. He opened his eyes and looked in amazement at the vibrant cloth in his hands. It contained a print of a beautiful snake pattern. The colours were earth browns, oranges, creams and yellows and the snake was painted in millions of little dots.

"It's beautiful, Gran!" he breathed.

Alice sat back comfortably in the chair by his bed. "It's an Aboriginal painting," she said. Clasping her hands together, she began to speak in a quiet voice:

"This is the story of the Rainbow serpent. Now, at the beginning of the world, in Dreamtime, it was dark. Nothing grew. Nothing moved. Everything was still and quiet. All the birds, animals and reptiles were still asleep under the ground. Then one day, the Rainbow Serpent awoke. She came to the surface and looked all around. She was really huge. Everywhere she went she left behind a winding track in the earth. Wherever she went to sleep, she left a deep hollow.

After a while the Rainbow Serpent grew lonely and wanted someone to talk to. She decided to wake up the other creatures."

"I don't blame her," muttered Bunda. "I wouldn't want to be on my own either."

"Well!" said Gran, "the first creatures she happened upon were the big-bellied frogs. Their stomachs were full of water they had stored up. They were so fat that they could hardly hop! They looked so funny that the Rainbow Serpent laughed to see them. Then she glanced around at the earth. The world was dry and barren. There weren't any rivers or lakes so no plants or trees could grow.

The Serpent sighed to herself for she knew that she was being selfish. She couldn't ask the other animals to share such a dreary place with her. Then, as the Rainbow Serpent looked at the frogs, she had an idea. She tickled the frogs' fat bellies with her forked tongue. At first it had no effect but then they began to smile. Then they began to snigger.

Finally, they began to howl with laughter. They laughed and laughed so much that the water inside them cascaded out. Soon the tracks and hollows made by the Rainbow Serpent were filled with bright, shining water. Yet the Serpent was not done with her tickling so the frog's helpless laughter continued to echo across the land. And, as long as they laughed the waters kept gushing from their mouths until all the rivers in Australia were formed. Plants and trees began to shoot up where nothing had grown before. Instead of just brown rocks and sand, the world became a kaleidoscope of colour.

Then the creatures came up from under the ground. At first they were shy and silent and crept timorously into the light. But, as the beauty of the Earth filled their eyes, each creature, according to its kind, roared, howled, barked, squawked or squeaked with delight.

Then the cavalcade of creatures leapt, galloped, jumped, rolled, hopped, slithered, scuttled or scampered with glee. The taste of freedom filled their heads and hearts with joy and they all agreed to live together in peace and harmony.

But soon things started to go wrong and the animals began to argue and fight and plot and plan against each other.

The Rainbow Serpent watched in horror as the animals became bitter enemies and learnt to hunt and kill.

All she had wanted was company and, in return, had given the earth and its creatures the gift of beauty. But when she saw she was powerless to stop the animals quarrelling, the Rainbow Serpent slipped sadly back under the ground never to return."

Gran finished her story and looked down at her grandson. His breathing was quiet and steady. He was fast asleep, the brightly coloured cloth clasped in his hand. Smoothing his black shiny hair with her hand, she smiled down on him and, turning out the light, she tiptoed from the room.

Chapter 3

How the World was Illuminated by a Bonfire

"Time for bed, Bunda," called his mother.

"Cool!" shouted Bunda, bounding up the stairs. Samantha looked at her mother in amazement. "Can this be the same boy?" she laughed. "You are having a wonderful effect on him, Mum."

"He loves stories," Alice smiled. "And I love telling them."

"Could I join you both for story time tonight?" asked Samantha.

"Of course you can come and listen, love," smiled Alice.

The two women walked companionably upstairs together. Alice collected a wrapped parcel from her room. When they reached Bunda's bedroom, he was sitting up in bed, arms folded and an excited look on his face.

"You're not at school now, Bunda," laughed his mother. Bunda giggled and relaxed against the pillows. His eyes shone expectantly as Gran carefully placed the parcel in his outstretched hands. Eagerly tearing it open, Bunda pulled out a hand puppet painted in dazzling colours.

It was a strange looking bird with a big beak. Bunda slipped his hand inside the puppet and made the bird open it's beak. It looked so funny that everyone laughed.

"This is a kookaburra," chuckled Gran, "a very famous Australian bird. This is his story."

Bunda, Samantha and the kookaburra puppet settled back to enjoy the tale.

"In the Dreamtime," said Gran, "there were no humans on earth, only animals. There was no sun, so everything was in darkness. Then, two birds, the crane and the emu, had a fierce argument. They squabbled and fought for days and days. In the end, the crane took one of the emu's eggs from her nest and, with all her strength, hurled it into the air. The egg hurtled past the clouds. Then, just when it seemed as if it would fly on up into the sky forever it hit a pile of firewood and smashed open. The egg yolk dripped onto the wood and set it alight. The fire blazed hot, and the huge flames lit up the world.

Down on earth, the animals were amazed because the world was light. For the first time they could see. A good spirit was watching over the animals. He could see how happy the animals were with the gift of sight and this gave him an idea.

With the help of his friends, the other spirits, he could light a bonfire every morning in the sky so that the animals on earth would never again have to stumble around in the darkness.

The spirits were happy to oblige, and soon they had collected an enormous amount of wood. But now the good spirit was worried that the animals might be frightened by the sudden blaze of light, so he lit the first morning star to warn them that the fire was about to start. Unfortunately, the animals were still asleep when the star appeared so they missed it altogether. The good spirit sent for Kookaburra.

"Kookaburra," he said, "you have the loudest voice of all the animals. Please will you watch for the morning star then sing with all your voice to wake up the other animals?"

Kookaburra was proud and pleased to be asked, and puffed out his feathered chest importantly.

The next day, when the morning star appeared in the velvety sky, Kookaburra opened his huge beak and started to sing. In truth it was a dreadful noise, but it did the trick and all the animals stirred, stretched and opened their sleepy eyes. They gazed up in awe at the beautiful morning star.

When they had the animals' attention the spirits lit the bonfire and the animals watched as the sky turned from black to grey then to pink and red.

Finally the fire's blaze was so great that it lit up the whole earth. The animals loved the light and the warmth that the fire created. They noticed that they felt hotter at mid-day, and the heat went out of the bonfire towards the end of the day. They knew this was because the good spirit was letting the blaze die down in readiness for the animal's sleep time.

Every morning from that day to this, Kookaburra has woken up the animals when the morning star appears in the sky.

Then Gran put a stern look on her face. "When people started to live on the earth, mothers told their children not to laugh at Kookaburra," she said, "even though he did look funny with his great big beak and his loud sharp voice."

Mothers would say, "If you laugh at the kookaburra, he might go away. Then the sun won't come up any more," Gran concluded. She smiled at Bunda. "Do you think this is true?" she asked him.

Bunda pretended to be listening to the kookaburra puppet that he was holding to his ear. "Kookaburra says it's true," he replied, "so I guess it must be!" Then Bunda gave an enormous yawn and, still wearing the kookaburra puppet on his hand, Bunda snuggled down under the duvet. "Goodnight," he murmured sleepily.

Gran and Mum smiled at each other and began to tiptoe out of the room.

"Gou - gour - gah - gah!"

shrieked Kookaburra.

Turning round in surprise, they saw the puppet waving a wing at them. Bunda was watching them through screwed up eyes, a mischievous smile on his face!

⚿ Chapter 4 ⚿

The Dreaming

The next evening at 7 o'clock, Bunda's Dad, Jack, arrived home from work.

"DAD!" roared Bunda, "you're home early! Cool!"

Samantha pretended to faint with shock and everyone laughed. Jack went over to Alice, sitting in her chair close to the fire.

"Hi, Alice," he said softly. Reaching down he kissed her old wrinkled cheek. "Great to see you home with your family, love," murmured Alice.

"So what's up?" joked Samantha. "Got the sack or something?"

"No!" Dad grinned at them all then he looked thoughtful for a moment and said, "Actually something has come up so I'll need to talk to you later. A big decision's got to be made!"

Bunda flung himself at his father. "Can we play my new computer game? Will you look at my painting of the Rainbow Snake?

Can we go outside and play football?"

"STOP!" laughed his father, trying to fend him off. "Let me get my jacket off first!"

Later on, when the excitement had died down and Bunda was on his way to bed, Jack said to Alice, "Bunda's been telling me about your stories, mum. Can I come to story time tonight?"

"Sure can," said Alice. "The more the merrier!"

Bunda was bouncing on his bed, singing at the top of his voice.

"Bunda, calm down!" said Samantha. "You'll break the bed, or have an accident, or both!"

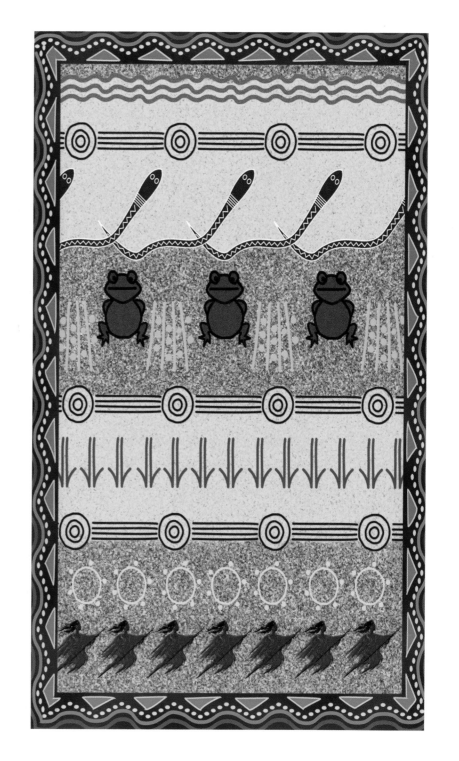

Alice approached the bed and took up her position in the chair. In her hands was a heavy, oddly shaped package, which she handed to Bunda.

"Oooh Gran," whispered Bunda.
"Thank you."

He tore at the wrapping paper on the present then carefully lifted out a clay model of a kangaroo. It was beautifully made and very lifelike.

"This is a totem, Bunda," said his grandmother. "All Aboriginal people have them."

"What's a totem?" asked Bunda.

"A totem is a special thing that keeps Aboriginals safe, happy, truthful and honest. It's a bit like a 'good luck' charm or a St Christopher pendant," explained Gran. "But they are usually creatures of one sort or another. They come from the Dreamtime. Aborigines used to travel from waterhole to waterhole, from one hunting ground to another. They were not just wandering aimlessly, they were following old paths taken by their Dreamtime Ancestors.

The Ancestors took many forms. Some were animals, some were stars and moons, trees and plants. They travelled around the unformed earth. When they paused, they left marks of their presence and when they finally reached the end of their journeys they changed into parts of the landscape, or disappeared into waterholes. Aboriginals believe that the Ancestors left something of themselves in these places.

Aboriginals get their totems from being born near a place where an Ancestor turned into a part of the landscape."

Gran fell silent and her eyes took on a faraway look. Silence shimmered in the air and, for a moment, it seemed as if they were all holding their breath. Then Bunda broke the spell by demanding that Gran told the story of his kangaroo.

"My grandmother once told me a story," said Gran. "There was a kangaroo who was very proud of his legs. They were long and strong and with them he could bound and leap almost as high as the sky.

Sadly, the other animals were not pleased with him and they complained to the spirits.

'Kangaroo doesn't look before he leaps,' said the duck-billed platypus. 'Only yesterday he came crashing down from out of the clouds and just missed smashing the eggs in my nest!'

'You think that's bad?' snapped the eagle. 'Well, let me tell you he nearly knocked me out of the sky when I was flying along minding my own business.'

'It's not right!' muttered all the other birds. 'Only creatures with feathers should be allowed to fly.'

The spirits frowned and shook their fists at Kangaroo. 'You are an evil creature,' they said.

'No I'm not!' retorted Kangaroo. 'I'm just high-spirited and maybe a little bit clumsy. I don't mean to do anybody any harm.'

'Nevertheless,' said the spirits. 'You cannot be allowed to go on causing trouble. From this day on you must walk and not jump.'

Kangaroo did not think this was fair and said so.

'Very well,' said the spirits, 'if you can leap from here to the shining sea before the sun sets we will allow you to go on jumping. But, be warned, if you fail we shall turn you into a rock!

Gran sighed and shook her head. "Kangaroo was foolish," she murmured. "He should have known that not even his powerful legs could jump so far in so little time. However, his pride would not let him turn down the challenge so he leapt forward with all his might. He jumped and bounced and tried his best to reach the ocean. But by the time the sun was setting and the first stars appearing in the evening sky, Kangaroo had still not reached the shining sea. Yet, Kangaroo could smell the salt and hear the waves crashing on the beach. Using all his remaining strength he took one last giant leap but he fell short and so the spirits turned him into a rock. But his brave effort had softened their hearts a little for, although they never turned him back into a kangaroo, they did allow all the other kangaroos to hop instead of walk."

"That's a sad story, Gran," said Bunda. Then he brightened up.
"Will my Kangaroo totem help me do well in my SAT's tests?"
he inquired hopefully.

"Sorry, love," laughed Gran, "only hard work and practice will do that
for you!"

Bunda's face fell for a moment then he began bouncing on his bed again.
"Look, I'm a kangaroo!" shouted Bunda. "The spirits will never stop me
from leaping as high as I like."

"Bunda, behave!" said his mother sternly.

Dad pulled a face at Bunda, mouthing the same words as Samantha.

"Dad, will you come home early every night?" yelled Bunda. "It's really
cool us all being together."

"I'll try, love," said Dad. "I'll definitely try."

◈ Chapter 5 ◈

Seven Sisters

As had become his custom ever since his Gran had arrived from Australia, Bunda sat up in bed waiting for her to come to tell him his story.

He looked at the wonderful gifts she'd bought him. He'd pinned up both his picture and the material printed Rainbow Serpent on his wall, while the clay kangaroo and kookaburra puppet were in places of honour on the shelf. A carved wooden boomerang, used as a hunting weapon by the Aborigines in the old days, was also one of Bunda's prized possessions.

In the corner of his room stood a huge didgeridoo. Slipping out of bed, he picked up the didgeridoo and blew a long deep mournful note on it. It had taken him two weeks to learn how to get a sound out of it.

"Blow a big fat raspberry down it," his Gran had instructed, but all that came out had been the sound of a cow in pain (at least that was how his

Dad had described it) and Bunda's lips and cheeks had tingled with the effort.

One day, though, he'd got the knack. A low, soft, mellow sound came out of the didgeridoo. Bunda was really proud of himself. He'd been driving the family mad with it ever since!

A sudden thought came into Bunda's head. He sighed and his head drooped. Tonight would be the last story from Gran. She was going back to Australia tomorrow. Bunda's throat ached with trying to hold back tears.

"I mustn't let Gran know I'm sad," he whispered to himself.

"Mum said it would make Gran upset and we don't want that."

Slow footsteps on the stairs indicated that Gran was coming up for story time. Bunda swallowed his tears and put on a brave smile to welcome her.

"G'day Bunda," laughed Alice. "Ready for the last story?"

"Yes, Gran, only…"

"What love?" questioned Alice, looking down at her grandson with love in her eyes.

"I… I… I'm soooo sad that you're going."

Bunda forgot to be brave and flung himself into his Gran's arms, sobbing as if his heart would break.

Gran held him close. "Don't cry, Bunda, we may be together sooner than you think!" she smiled knowingly. "Well, are you ready for the story?"

Bunda sniffed loudly, dried his tears on the sleeve of his pyjamas and looked for his gift.

"Where is it Gran?" he asked.

"Tonight you get your gift at the end of the story," said Gran. "Now hop into bed and I'll begin… This is a story about seven sisters who lived in the Dreamtime. They were very beautiful, with long flowing hair. Their bodies sparkled with icicles. They were called the Meamei, and were brave and strong hunters.

The sisters were loved by seven brothers called the Berai-Berai, the honey hunters. The brothers wanted to marry the Meamei, but the sisters were not in love with them and refused their advances.

The poor brothers tried everything to persuade them to change their minds including finding sweet honeycombs for them. But the hard-hearted sisters only ate the honey then laughed at the Berai-Berai.

Now it is said that pride often goes before a fall and so it was with these cruel girls. Unfortunately for them, the Fiery Ancestor, Wurrunnah also wanted the sisters for himself. However, he had no intention of wasting his time wooing the Meamei like the lovelorn brothers. No, he put his faith in cunning and trickery and so he laid an ambush for them.

He roared in triumph when they fell into his trap but he was mistaken if he thought that their capture would bring him joy.

The sisters struggled and fought against him, and eventually he had enough of them. 'If you can't love me,' he cried in fury, 'then I shall make sure no one can have you!' So saying he put five of them in the sky as shining stars.

However, he couldn't bear to part with all the sisters so he kept the two most beautiful as his prisoners. Despite his anger and disappointment he could not resist staring at them and trying to put his arms around them. But the flames that danced around Wurrunnah caused their icicles to melt.

The chill water poured over him and doused his fire. He howled in rage and disgust, for Wurrunnah, the fiery ancestor, was fiery no more. Madness seized the mind of Wurrunnah and he hurled the two women into the sky to join their sisters. Now everyone could see their beauty but they were cold and distant and forever out of reach."

Gran sighed wistfully then she continued.
"The seven beautiful star sisters became the cluster we call the Pleiades. If you look up in the sky and find them, Bunda, you will see that the two sisters whose icicles were melted by Wurrunnah's fire do not shine as brightly as the others. It was their fate to be the most loved and the most cursed."

Gran shook her head slowly then looked sadly at Bunda. "But what, you might ask, happened to the poor Berai-Berai?

Well, they were heartbroken to lose their beautiful Meamei. They no longer found joy in hunting and so, without food, they starved to death.

However, the spirits felt such great love should never die and so they carried the brothers up into the heavens to be with the seven sisters. Now the Berai-Berai can be seen as the belt and sword of Orion.

So you see, Bunda, even the saddest stories can have a happy ending." Gran nodded her head thoughtfully. Then she smiled a secret smile before she continued with the story.

"The brothers still hunt for honey in the sky, and the Meamei still sing beautiful songs. Sometimes they break bits off their icicles and throw them down to earth where they land in the form of early morning frost. When the Aboriginals see the frost, they know that the Meamei haven't forgotten them. When it thunders they think it is the Meamei jumping into water, playing at who can make the biggest splash. This means that rain is on its way!"

Bunda was silent for a moment when Gran finished speaking, then in a swift movement, jumped out of bed and ran to the window.

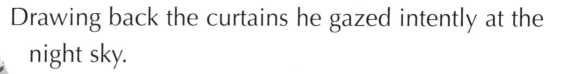

Drawing back the curtains he gazed intently at the night sky.

"So Gran," he said thoughtfully, "I can see the seven sisters and the honey hunters when it's night time in England, and you can see the same stars when it's night time in Australia!"

"Well, that's not going to happen Bunda," said Gran, "but it's a lovely idea."

Bunda turned back to his grandmother. His face was downcast.
"I thought that might be our happy ending," he whispered miserably.

"I thought at least we could look at the same stars."

Before his Gran could reply, Bunda's father stepped into the room. Bunda saw the smiling face of his mother peeping round his father's back.

"Mum, I think you should give Bunda his last present now," said Dad mysteriously.

"Yessss! What is it? What's my present?" shouted Bunda, beside himself with excitement, holding out his hands expectantly.

"I haven't got anything to give you," said Gran.

Bunda's face fell.

"However, I have got something to tell you," smiled Gran. "We will be able to look at the stars together after all because… your Dad's been offered a job in Australia and you're all coming to Perth to live with me!!"

Bunda's mouth fell open in amazement.

"But… but what about Mum's teaching job?" he stammered.

"I've made enquiries, and I can get a teaching job out there," answered his mother smiling so brightly that Gran thought that not even the seven sisters could have outshone her.

Bunda's face went through a range of emotions starting with shock, quickly followed by disbelief, then by an enormous flood of joy and happiness that filled his whole body.

His grin spread wider and wider. He thought he would burst with excitement as he flung himself into his Gran's arms.

The chill water poured over him and doused his fire. He howled in rage and disgust, for Wurrunnah, the fiery ancestor, was fiery no more. Madness seized the mind of Wurrunnah and he hurled the two women into the sky to join their sisters. Now everyone could see their beauty but they were cold and distant and forever out of reach."

Gran sighed wistfully then she continued.
"The seven beautiful star sisters became the
cluster we call the Pleiades. If you look up in the
sky and find them, Bunda, you will see that the two
sisters whose icicles were melted by Wurrunnah's
fire do not shine as brightly as the others.
It was their fate to be the most loved
and the most cursed."

Gran shook her head slowly
then looked sadly at
Bunda. "But what,
you might ask,
happened to the
poor Berai-Berai?

Well, they were heartbroken to lose their beautiful Meamei. They no longer found joy in hunting and so, without food, they starved to death.

However, the spirits felt such great love should never die and so they carried the brothers up into the heavens to be with the seven sisters. Now the Berai-Berai can be seen as the belt and sword of Orion.

So you see, Bunda, even the saddest stories can have a happy ending." Gran nodded her head thoughtfully. Then she smiled a secret smile before she continued with the story.

"The brothers still hunt for honey in the sky, and the Meamei still sing beautiful songs. Sometimes they break bits off their icicles and throw them down to earth where they land in the form of early morning frost. When the Aboriginals see the frost, they know that the Meamei haven't forgotten them. When it thunders they think it is the Meamei jumping into water, playing at who can make the biggest splash. This means that rain is on its way!"

Bunda was silent for a moment when Gran finished speaking, then in a swift movement, jumped out of bed and ran to the window.

"Cool," he whispered. "Stories every night for ever and ever and ever!"